LITTLE MISS BIRTHDAY

originated by Roger Hargreaves

Written and illustrated by Adam Hargreaves

MR. MEN   **LITTLE MISS**

PSS!

PRICE STERN SLOAN

An Imprint of Penguin Group (USA) Inc.

Little Miss Birthday™ and copyright © 2006 by THOIP (a Sanrio company). All rig...
First published in the United States in 2007 by Price Stern Sloan, a division of Penguin
Young Readers Group, 345 Hudson Street, New York, New York 10014. *PSS!* is a
registered trademark of Penguin Group (USA) Inc. Manufactured in China.

The publisher does not have any control over and does not assume any
responsibility for author or third-party websites or their content.

ISBN 978-0-8431-2131-5

23 22 21 20 19 18

Little Miss Birthday enjoys every day because every day is someone's birthday and Little Miss Birthday loves birthday presents! She loves choosing presents, she loves wrapping presents, and she loves giving presents.

And she is very good at choosing presents. Little Miss Birthday prides herself on always picking the perfect present.

However fussy the person may be.

Last year, she gave Mr. Fussy a tiny iron for ironing his shoelaces. It was exactly what he wanted. Nobody is sure if they have ever seen Mr. Fussy look quite so happy.

She gave Little Miss Star a radio that gives her a round of applause every time she turns it on.

And she gave Mr. Bump a bed with no legs. No more going bump in the night for Mr. Bump when he falls out of bed!

Little Miss Birthday has a birthday book to help her keep track of everyone's birthday.

A very big birthday book.

Last week, Little Miss Birthday was leafing through her book to see whose birthdays were coming up.

"Mr. Lazy," she read out loud. "Easy peasy. I will give Mr. Lazy an alarm clock with a silent alarm. Now, who is next? Mr. Wrong."

A puzzled expression settled across Little Miss Birthday's face. She could not think of anything to give to Mr. Wrong.

"Just think harder," she told herself.

But the harder she thought, the more puzzled she became. Little Miss Birthday did not have a clue what to give Mr. Wrong for his birthday.

Everything she could think of would be wrong!

The next day, she had plenty of time to ponder this problem because it was Little Miss Late's birthday and Little Miss Late, it won't surprise you to hear, was late for her own birthday.

When she finally turned up, she loved her present.

A bus stop.

No more running to the bus stop to catch the bus, she now always has one with her!

That night, Little Miss Birthday hardly slept a wink. Mr. Wrong's birthday was drawing closer and she still had no idea what to give him.

The following day, Little Miss Birthday decided that the simplest thing to do was to visit Mr. Wrong, and hope that would give her a few ideas.

Mr. Wrong lives in a house that . . . well, just looks wrong!

When Little Miss Birthday rang the doorbell, it did not go "ding-dong," it did not even buzz.

Do you know what noise it made?

It went: "OINK, OINK!"

"Come in, come in," said Mr. Wrong as he answered the door and promptly stepped outside.

Mr. Wrong and Little Miss Birthday made themselves comfortable in the garden.

They had a long conversation, none of which made any sense to Little Miss Birthday, but she did have a very nice time.

Though unfortunately, their chat left Little Miss Birthday no nearer to solving the problem of what to give Mr. Wrong as a birthday present.

The next day, Little Miss Birthday went out for a walk.

"What would Mr. Wrong want more than anything else?" she asked herself, watching the autumn leaves blowing past.

"Morning, Mr. Muddle," she said to Mr. Muddle, who was on his way to the shops. Or was he on his way back? He could never be sure.

"Afternoon," replied Mr. Muddle. "Lovely summer's day we're enjoying."

"But it's not summer . . ." said Little Miss Birthday, and then she had an idea.

"Of course! Thank you, Mr. Muddle," she cried, and rushed off to organize Mr. Wrong's birthday present.

A few days later, it was Mr. Wrong's birthday. Little Miss Birthday went around to Mr. Wrong's house with his present.

Mr. Wrong had heard the doorbell "OINK, OINK!" but he kept opening the wrong door.

He had opened the pantry door, the cupboard door, and the fridge door, before he finally opened the front door.

"Good-bye! Good-bye!" greeted Mr. Wrong.
He looked at Little Miss Birthday.

"You've brought me a present," he said. "It must
be . . ."

Before Mr. Wrong could utter another word, Little
Miss Birthday cried, "Merry Christmas!" and gave
him a present wrapped in Christmas paper.

Mr. Wrong stood holding the present in
astonishment.

"I was just about to say it must be Christmas! And . . . I was right!" he exclaimed.

Mr. Wrong was over the moon. Little Miss Birthday had given him the one thing he wanted more than anything else.

Mr. Wrong wanted to be right!

Mr. Wrong tore the wrapping paper off Little Miss Birthday's present.

She had given him a sled.

"It's fantastic!" cried Mr. Wrong. "I've always wanted a . . ."

". . . bike!"

Little Miss Birthday just smiled.